CLOUDY
with a chance of
MEAT BALLS 2™

FLINT AND FRIENDS!

adapted by Cordelia Evans
illustrated by Andre Medina

Ready-to-Read

Simon Spotlight

New York   London   Toronto   Sydney   New Delhi

Read the original book by
Judi Barrett and Ron Barrett.

SIMON SPOTLIGHT
An imprint of Simon & Schuster Children's Publishing Division
1230 Avenue of the Americas, New York, New York 10020
TM & © 2013 Sony Pictures Animation, Inc. All Rights Reserved.
SIMON SPOTLIGHT, READY-TO-READ, and colophon are registered trademarks of Simon & Schuster, Inc.
For information about special discounts for bulk purchases, please contact Simon & Schuster Special Sales at
1-866-506-1949 or business@simonandschuster.com.
Manufactured in the United States of America 1013 LAK
2 4 6 8 10 9 7 5 3
ISBN 978-1-4424-9553-1 (pbk)
ISBN 978-1-4424-9554-8 (hc)
ISBN 978-1-4424-9555-5 (eBook)

My name is Flint Lockwood,
and I am an inventor.
I invented a machine that turns
water into food.
Recently I saved my town,
Swallow Falls, from being destroyed
by my machine . . .
for the second time!

I could never have done it
without help from my friends.

But it took me a while
to realize that.

My friends are the bravest,
smartest people I know.
Even if they may not always
seem like it.

First there is Steve.
Steve is my lab partner
and the best friend I could ask for.
I invented a machine that lets him
say what he is thinking.
Usually he just says, "Steve!"

Then there is my dad, Tim.
I always thought I let him down
because I did not want to work at
his sardine bait and tackle shop.
But now I know that he believes in me,
even when my inventions
cause trouble.

My friend Earl is a police officer
in Swallow Falls.
He is very strong and tough,
but there is one thing he cannot break:
yellow police tape.

Brent was not always my friend.
He used to be a bully,
but it was only because he
did not know his own strength.
Now he is very loyal.
He is willing to do lots of
crazy things to help people.

When I first met Manny,
he was working as a cameraman.
Then I found out he has
many other talents.
He is an animal doctor, a cook,
a pilot, *and* an actor!

And then there is Sam Sparks.
Sam is a scientist
who studies the weather.
She is more than just a friend.

Sam and I have plans to get a place
where we work together.
We are going to call it Sparkswood.

I thought I had a new friend
when I met Chester V.
He is a great inventor and was my hero.

Chester and I have a lot in common.
We were both bullied
when we were kids.
Most importantly, we both invented
wedgie-proof underwear.

But it turned out Chester did not believe in friends.

You see, after Swallow Falls
was almost destroyed the first time
by my food machine,
Chester came to take all of us
to San Franjose while his company,
Live Corp, cleaned up our home.

A few months later, Chester told me
my food machine was still on the island.
In fact, he said, it was creating
living food that had
taken over the island!

Chester asked me to go
back to Swallow Falls.
He wanted me to destroy my machine
and all its food animal creations.

Of course I asked my friends
to come with me!
We all set sail in Dad's boat
for Swallow Falls.

When we got there,
Sam made friends with
one of the food animals,
a sweet strawberry she named Barry.

The more food animals we met,
the more Sam and my friends
started to think that maybe the
living food was not dangerous after all.

But I did not believe them.
I believed Chester.
He said the animals were dangerous.
I left my friends to help him
on his mission to find my machine.

My friends said
I could not destroy my machine.
It was creating friendly,
harmless creatures.

Then a group of friendly marshmallows
saved my life.
I realized my friends were right!

It turned out that Chester did not
want to destroy the machine either.

He wanted to use it
to create delicious food bars!
Chester said he would turn my friends
into food bars if I did not let him
have my food machine.

With the help of Steve
and one of my inventions,
I saved my friends
from Chester's plan.

And then they helped me
catch Chester before he escaped
with my food machine.

Chester did not have any friends
to help him when he was in trouble.

Chester made me think that my friends
were holding me back.
He thought that to be
a good inventor you had to
go through life without friends.
But he was wrong.

My old friends and
my new friends are way more
important to me than any invention!